NIGHT BOAT TO FREEDOM

It was in 1863, and one night I carried across about twelve on the same night. Somebody must have seen us, because they set out after me as soon as I stepped out of the boat back on the Kentucky side; from that time on they were after me.

—Arnold Gragston
His account and others in the
WPA's *Slave Narrative Collection* were
the inspiration for this book.

Night Boat to Freedom

MARGOT THEIS RAVEN   Pictures by E. B. LEWIS

SQUARE
FISH

Farrar Straus Giroux

If I close my eyes, I can still remember being a boy in the pineboard cabin where I was born on Christmas morning and got my name, Christmas John.

I can see the river, too, that swept wide by old master's Big House in Kentucky, keepin' us a boat trip away from Ohio and freedom.

But mostly I can see Granny Judith, who raised me from a baby, bending over her dye pots, boiling and stirring up hanks of thread.

I can see her hanging thread out to dry, then taking a hank of it to weave up in the loom house. Weave it into a color of the rainbow coming from her old pot. Indigo dying pretty blue. Bay leaves, sun yellow. Pine straw making purple.

And bamboo turning turkey red, the color that stole Granny Judith from Africa and put her in slavery.

One night by pinewood light, Granny Judith told me the story of the strangers who came to her village and laid down a red flannel cloth in front of her. It was so pretty she grabbed for it, but they tricked her on and on with bigger pieces till they got her across a river and onto a ship.

"Lord, child," Granny Judith cried, "when that ship sailed away, I wept to go home, but the ship sailed on—across the ocean—and the pretty color of red turned the sad color of slavery for me."

Then Granny Judith spoke so low even the dark couldn't hear her. "But now, Christmas John, we got a chance to learn the color of freedom! A man across the river has a station for escapin' slaves. Cook's child, Molly, can go to him by boat tomorrow when the moon's black. I'm askin' you to take her."

I grew so quiet you could've heard a sewin' needle fall on feathers. I was twelve summers grown and a strong hulk of a boy, but I felt feeble as a baby knowin' what she wanted me to do.

"I know you got fear, child," Granny Judith said, "but what scares the head is best done with the heart. Master lets you go about 'cause you're young yet. You can slip over and back before mornin' star come, and I'll be here prayin' and waitin' to know what color Molly wore to freedom."

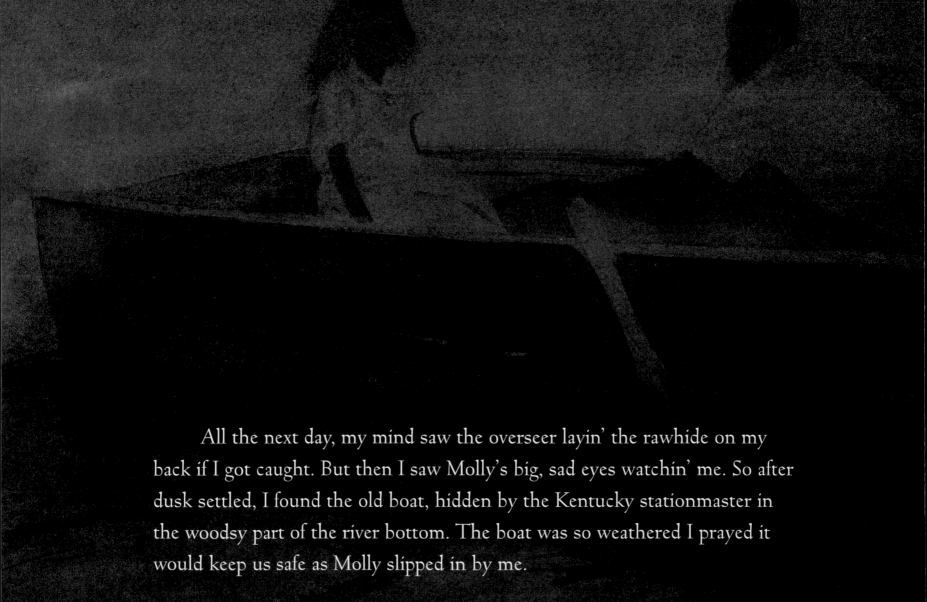

All the next day, my mind saw the overseer layin' the rawhide on my back if I got caught. But then I saw Molly's big, sad eyes watchin' me. So after dusk settled, I found the old boat, hidden by the Kentucky stationmaster in the woodsy part of the river bottom. The boat was so weathered I prayed it would keep us safe as Molly slipped in by me.

It was black-dark and I couldn't see her, but I felt her eyes. We didn't risk to speak. I just rowed in the cold, prayin' nobody would hear my oars slap-slappin' through the water. The current pulled hard, and my heart pounded. All I knew 'bout the Ohio side was to row toward a lighthouse and a ringin' bell. Would patrollers with whips be there waitin' for us?

Finally, I saw a tall light and pulled to it. Two men appeared from the shadows. One grabbed for the girl, the other for me! I thought we were caught till a foghorn voice asked me, "You hungry, boy?"

I shook my head no, unable to speak. Then I figured those men had to be the Ohio stationmasters! Just before I pushed off, I remembered to ask Molly what color dress she was wearin'.

"Blue" came back her whispered answer. It was the only word she said all night. Later, when I told it to Granny Judith in our cabin, it made her smile somethin' beautiful!

After that first trip, I didn't sleep easy for weeks. Then I saw no one was any the wiser to what I'd done. By and by, I got to like the idea of helpin' others cross the river. Granny Judith did, too, sayin' as long as we had each other, we'd get by where we were a bit longer. Soon I was making three and four trips a month. Sometimes I took two people. Sometimes a whole boatload. They'd meet me in the open on the black nights of the moon and give me a password from the Bible—"*Menare.*"

Then I'd row them across the river, in that old boat that became my friend. Night after night it kept me and my secret safe as I'd hurry back in the dark—boat and me making it to shore just as the mornin' star lit the sky.

"What color is freedom tonight, Christmas John?" Granny Judith'd ask when I'd sneak back into our cabin. I'd tell her yellow, indigo, green—the colors worn by people in the night, people I could touch but never see.

One day, I saw Granny Judith cookin' up colors in her old pot, dying cloth. She said she had a dream-vision to make a quilt and stretch out the freedom colors in pretty squares like a rainbow bridge from side to side.

"When there's only two squares left to finishin', our work will be done here. Then, Christmas John"—she shivered, leanin' closer—"dream says we got to get ourselves over the river, 'cause the danger's gonna grow awful."

Black moon by black moon, I made the river trips, and square by square, Granny Judith's quilt grew. Soon a whole year had passed. Master had me workin' in the fields now, and I had to take bigger chances to sneak off.

Then one night 'bout July, when the green corn was ripe enough to eat, I stepped out of the boat and heard bloodhounds bayin' close by! I hid up a tree, shakin' so badly I could hardly hold on till the dogs left. Thank the Lord Granny Judith had sewn little pouches stuffed with ground-up Indian turnip and tied them on my feet! The root smelled like strong pepper and kept the dogs from knowin' my scent.

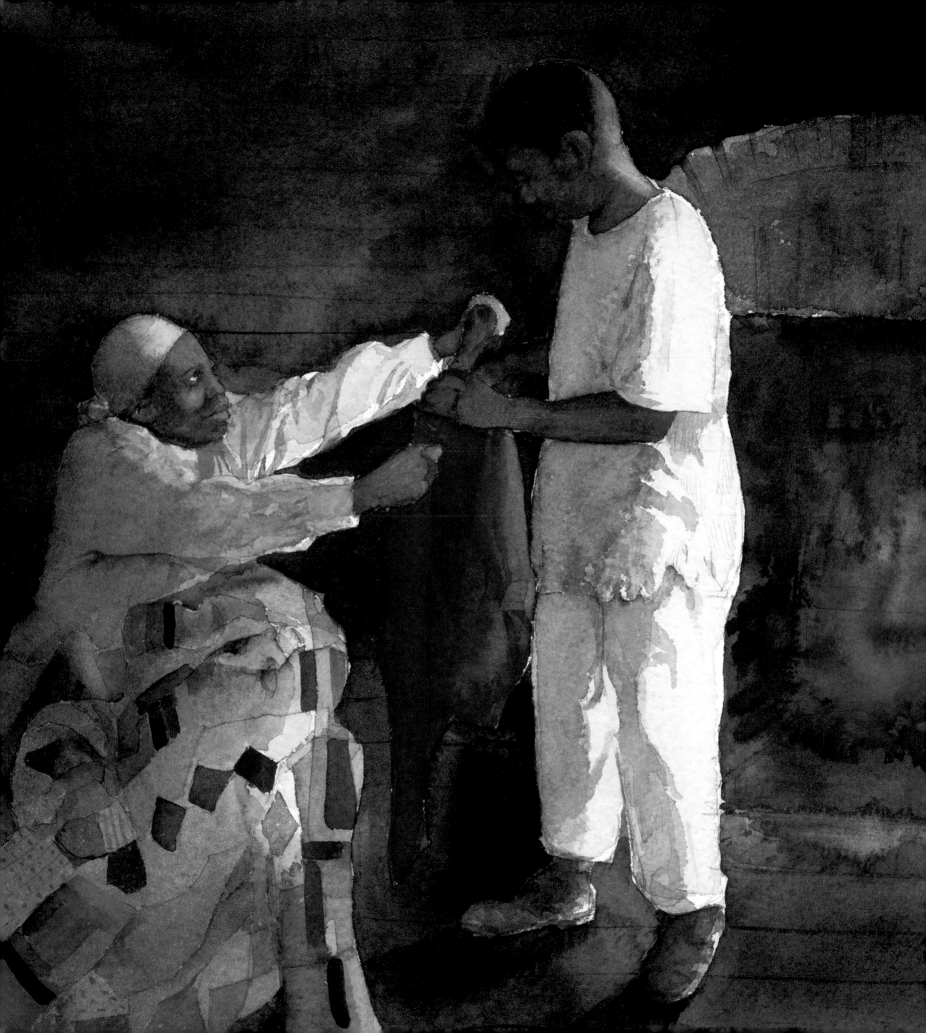

"You'd surely been killed!" Granny Judith cried when I told her about the dogs. Then she held the quilt in the pine knot light. There were only two squares missin' to bridge the cloth end to end.

"Put this on," Granny Judith said as she handed me a fine new shirt she'd woven and dyed. In the low light, her needle jumped silver, up and down, as she sewed a new patch on the quilt. It was the color of my shirt. Turkey red.

"It's your freedom color"—she smiled—" 'cause tonight you've got to row yourself to safety, Christmas John."

"But where's your quilt patch, Granny Judith?" I asked. "We're goin' together."

"That's foolish talk, child," she said, and shook her head. "Mornin' star's nearly here and those dogs are all about. I'd just get you caught . . . slow you down."

Granny Judith put the near-finished quilt into my hands and pressed her cheek to mine. "You take my night colors to the freedom side where they belong, and don't you cry for me, Christmas John"—her voice grew strong— " 'cause love don't stop at a river, and no river's wide enough to keep us apart."

Then she hugged me hard and gentled me out the door with my heart achin' till I thought it would burst.

I tore off faster than a wild horse into the woods, but near some muddy ground my feet slowed. A breeze fanned my face. I looked to the sky. No mornin' star yet! No dogs! How could I leave Granny Judith?

"Freedom's got no color for me without you," I said, openin' the cabin door and grabbin' for her. I could feel her tremblin', so I put her hand to my beatin' chest. "What scares the head is best done with the heart. Let me take you across."

"Praise God, child, your heart's brave enough for both of us." Her eyes tendered. Then she stood to come with me.

Quiet as we could, we cut our way through the woods. Then I heard the dogs start up again.

Mornin' star rose in the purple night as I got us to the boat. We slipped over its side and headed for the light and the bell. I pulled the oars hard. Behind me I heard the bloodhounds. Slave hunters with guns and torches swept the water for us. I rowed harder, praying to hear the sound of that bell. The night stayed quiet for the longest time. Then I heard it—the bell! But no matter how hard I rowed, land didn't get any closer.

Finally, I saw the spill of the lighthouse beam in the river. I rowed my boat toward it. Just when I thought I'd collapse, we reached shore—Ohio!

Friendly arms and the foghorn voice helped us to the dock. Sweat ran down our faces, and Granny Judith cried, shakin' from fear and joy.

I wrapped the quilt around her like a big warm hug and touched the one empty patch on the cloth. Then, with the last of my breath, I asked her the question she'd asked me so many times: "What color is freedom tonight?"

"Oh, Lord, child!" She let out a great song of a laugh. "Didn't my dye pot teach you anythin' 'bout colors? Look at us, Christmas John," she cried, holdin' up her arms to the last whisper of night. "In the dark of the moon we are *all* the colors of freedom, sugar! You and me, child! You and me!"

Slowly, pink mornin' cracked the sky. Behind us the water lapped against the dock. I turned one last time to see my weathered old friend, the boat that'd brought us—and so many others—across the river to freedom.

In that new day risin', I watched it rock peaceful as a babe's cradle that's done its work for the night.

AUTHOR'S NOTE

"May the morning star greet you on your prayin' ground" was a protective blessing offered by one slave to another when secret worship meetings were held in the woods at night. At the sight of the morning star, the brightest light to show itself in the sky just before dawn, the gathered slaves knew to return home quickly lest they be caught.

Such rich knowledge of slave life within the plantation system can be learned from reading a remarkable body of work called the *Slave Narrative Collection*, which was compiled during the Great Depression of the 1930s, when the Federal Writers' Project gave jobless writers the task of interviewing ex-slaves who had been children during the last years of slavery. Many were in their eighties and nineties, some well over a hundred, when interviewed. In all, more than two thousand first-person histories were recorded.

After reading hundreds and hundreds of these accounts, I began to hear certain voices from the past reaching out to share their particular stories with me. A young male slave born on Christmas morning told of his courageous trips across the river flowing between the slave state of Kentucky and the Free State of Ohio. For almost four years he rowed others at night, not freeing himself until the risk of being caught grew too strong. The details of the stationmaster's lighthouse and bell, the mysterious password the escaping slaves used, and the pitch-dark nights on which he traveled all came from his account.

Another narrative that captured my imagination was about a woman named Granny Judith. She was lured from her African village by pale-face strangers who repeatedly put an irresistible red cloth in front of her, moving it closer and closer to their slave ship so they could eventually get her on board. Granny Judith with her love of color became the inspiration for the character with the same name in *Night Boat to Freedom*.

Many plantations had women like Granny Judith who were artists with their dye pots, taking the raw materials of plants and roots to create beautiful colors that they then used in making cloth. I felt it was important to celebrate the artistic expression of the dye pot as a small light of freedom in a slave's dark world.

Finally, in the quilt that I envisioned Granny Judith making, I wanted to focus upon the love within a slave's family, and use Granny's sewing of the freedom squares to show that stitches of love and selflessness can be stronger than any chains that seek to enslave the human spirit.

Night Boat to Freedom is like Granny Judith's quilt: patches of truth stitched together by voices alive with history.

To Eloise Raven, a great lady with a great heart.
You are loved and missed.
—M.T.R.

A special thanks to Middleton Place, South Carolina.
—E.B.L.

SQUARE
FISH
An Imprint of Macmillan

NIGHT BOAT TO FREEDOM. Text copyright © 2006 by Margot Theis Raven.
Illustrations copyright © 2006 by E. B. Lewis.
All rights reserved. Printed in China.
For information, address Square Fish, 175 Fifth Avenue, New York, N.Y. 10010.

Square Fish and the Square Fish logo are trademarks of Macmillan
and are used by Farrar, Straus and Giroux under license from Macmillan.

Originally published in the United States by Farrar, Straus and Giroux
Designed by Barbara Grzeslo
Square Fish logo designed by Filomena Tuosto
First Square Fish Edition: January 2009
10 9 8 7 6 5 4 3 2
www.squarefishbooks.com

Raven, Margot Theis.
Night boat to freedom / Margot Theis Raven ; pictures by E.B. Lewis.
p. cm.
Summary: At the request of his fellow slave Granny Judith, Christmas John risks his life to
take runaways across a river from Kentucky to Ohio. Based on slave narratives recorded in the 1930s.
ISBN-13: 978-0-312-55018-9
ISBN-10: 0-312-55018-9
[1. Fugitive slaves—Fiction. 2. Slavery—Fiction. 3. Underground railroad—Fiction.
4. African Americans—Fiction. 5. Kentucky—History—1792–1865—Fiction. 6. Ohio—
History—1787–1865—Fiction.] I. Lewis, Earl B., ill. II. Title.

PZ7.R1955 Chr 2006
[E]—dc22
2005042923

The quote on the title page from Arnold Gragston appears in the Florida volume of the WPA's *Slave Narrative Collection*, which can be found at the Library of Congress. Mr. Gragston was interviewed for the Federal Writers' Project when he was ninety-seven years old. He estimates that before he got freedom himself, he may have helped as many as two to three hundred other slaves find their way to freedom.